For Wendy – *C.P.*

For Hannah Lily Sunshine, with love – *J.M.*

The Sierra Club, founded in 1892 by John Muir, has devoted itself to the study and protection of the earth's scenic and ecological resources—mountains, wetlands, woodlands, wild shores and rivers, deserts and plains. The publishing program of the Sierra Club offers books to the public as a nonprofit educational service in the hope that they may enlarge the public's understanding of the Club's basic concerns. The point of view expressed in each book, however, does not necessarily represent that of the Club. The Sierra Club has some sixty chapters in the United States and in Canada. For information about how you may participate in its programs to preserve wilderness and the quality of life, please address inquiries to Sierra Club, 85 Second Street, San Francisco, CA 94105.

Text copyright © 1996 by Caroline Pitcher
Illustrations copyright © 1996 by Jackie Morris

First U.S. Edition 1996

The Snow Whale was designed and produced by Frances Lincoln Limited, 4 Torriano Mews, Torriano Avenue, London NW5 2RZ.

Library of Congress Cataloging-in-Publication data is available from Sierra Club Books for Children, 85 Second Street, San Francisco, CA 94105.

Printed in Hong Kong

10 9 8 7 6 5 4 3 2 1

The Snow Whale

by Caroline Pitcher

Illustrated by
Jackie Morris

Sierra Club Books for Children
San Francisco

One cold winter night, snow fell as fast and thick as down from a duck's back. In the morning, the hills were blanketed with snow.

Laurie ran into the garden and searched for a stick. She drew a huge shape in the hillside. Her brother Leo plowed through the snow after her, holding high his bucket and shovel.

"What shall I do?" he asked.
"Pile up the snow," she said.

"What are you building?"
"A whale."

"Where does the snow come from?" asked Leo.

His sister sighed. "Don't you know *anything*?" she said.
"The water rises up from the ocean and goes into the clouds.
Then it comes down again as rain or snow."

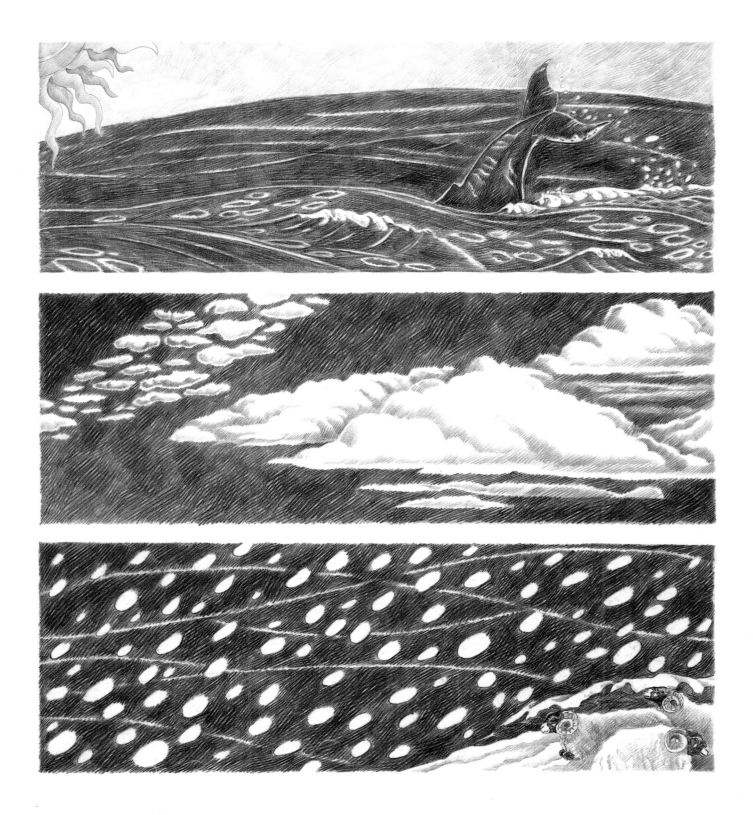

Out ran Nick from next door. He brought his wheelbarrow to help, and his sister Kate brought a garden rake.

"Where will the whale swim?" asked Leo.

Nobody answered. They were too busy huffing and puffing, bringing the whale out of the hill.

"Bring me the rake, Leo," said Laurie.
"Why?"
"To draw his tail flukes and his big filter mouth."
"But what will he eat?" asked Leo.
Nobody answered, so he brought her the rake.

"Bring me Dad's ladder, Leo," said Laurie.

"Why?"

"To climb up his back and make his blowhole."

"What will he blow?" asked Leo.

Nobody answered, so he went to get the ladder. On the way back, he found a special stone on the path.

"Here's the whale's eye!" he cried.
"It's very tiny," said Laurie.
"But it looks happy," said Leo, and he climbed up
to put it on the whale's face.

They shoveled and dug and bucketed and wheeled
and packed and patted and polished and smoothed.
Then they stood back and looked.

He was the most beautiful snow whale in the whole world—
high as a house, round as a cloud, white as an ice floe.

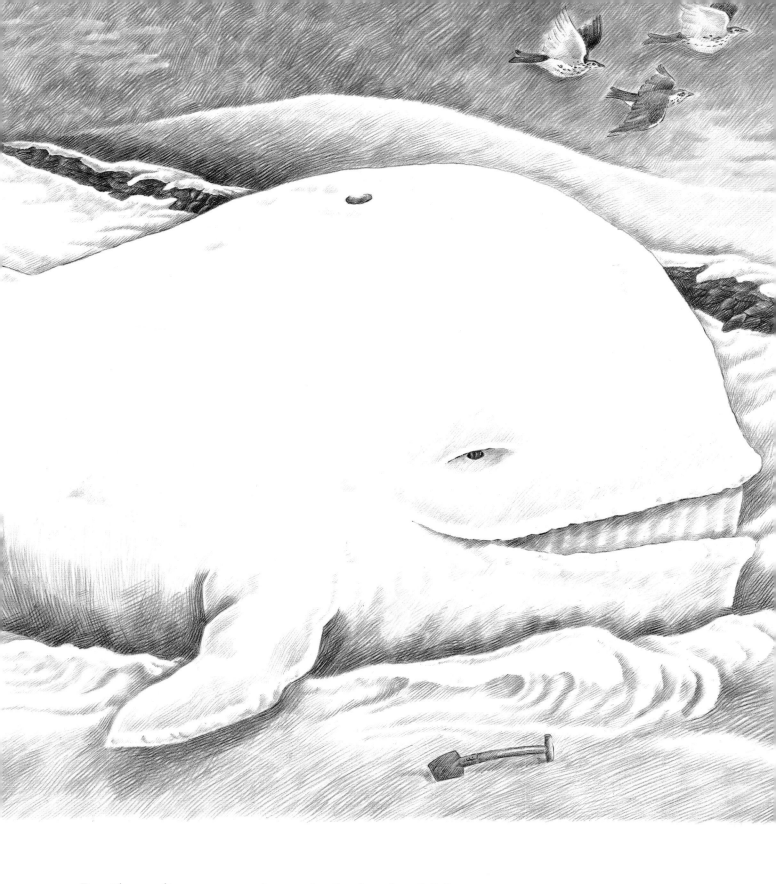

In the afternoon the whale looked blue.
"That's because he's freezing," said Laurie, "and so am I."

They ran home to thaw their fingers and to dry
their gloves and socks.

As darkness settled over the hillside, Laurie and Leo watched the whale from their window.

"If he sang, his voice would shatter the hills," whispered Laurie. "If he thrashed his tail, he would break our house in two."

The next day, it was so cold that the snow whale's mouth was full of icicles. The children played with him all day. They ran around him, climbed on his back, and slid down his sides.

They sailed him over the seven seas. They told him
stories about ants and elephants and made him smile.

Later, when the sun broke through and
water drops began to drip from the branches,
the snow whale glistened like silver.

"Where does the snow go?" asked Leo.

His sister sighed. "Don't you know *anything*?"
she said. "It melts and flows back into the rivers
and down into the ocean again."

That night, Leo dreamed of whales singing
and playing with their calves at the bottom
of the sea.

When he woke, someone was crying, but it wasn't the whale.
It was Laurie.

"Where has the whale gone?" she sobbed.

"I *do* know that," he said, putting his arms around her.
"He's gone back to the ocean again. Snow whale's gone home."